My First Book Of Patterns

Small Letters

Wonder House

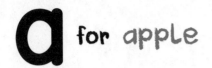 **for** apple

Color the letter **a** and the **apple** brightly.

apple

Trace the letter.

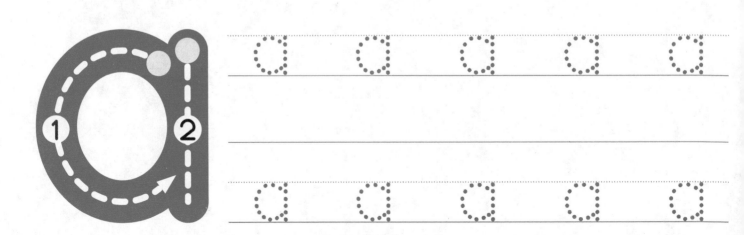

b for ball

Color the letter b and the ball brightly.

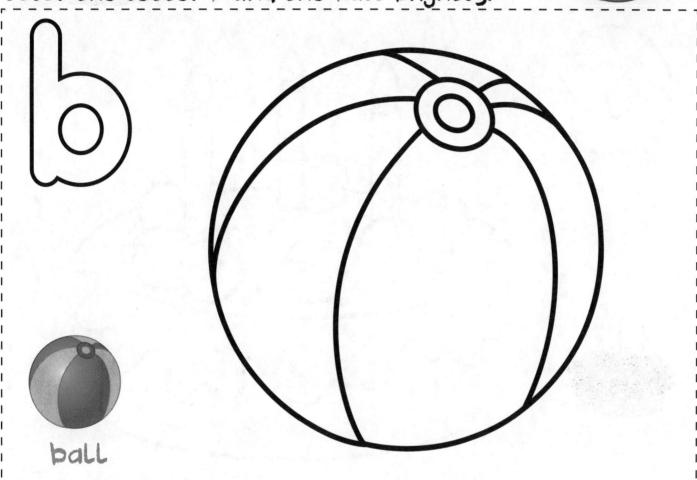

ball

Trace the letter.

b b b b b

b b b b b

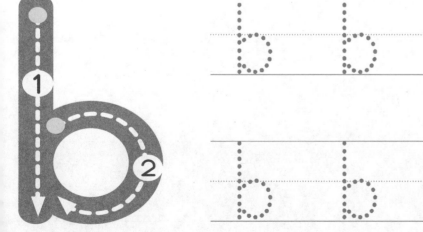

C for cake

Color the letter c and the cake brightly.

cake

Trace the letter.

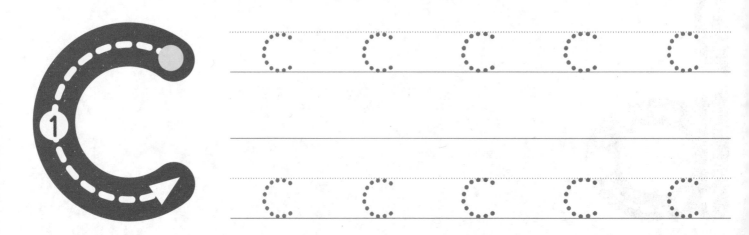

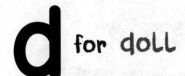 **d** for doll

Color the letter d and the doll brightly.

doll

Trace the letter.

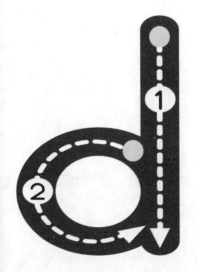

d d d d d

d d d d d

 for egg

Color the letter e and the eggs brightly.

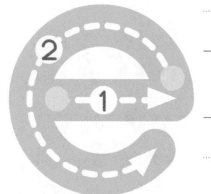
egg

Trace the letter.

Match Them Up!

Trace the given letters and match with the correct picture.

Find the First Letter!

Circle the beginning letter of each picture.

e a b

c e b

d e a

c a b

Circle the Matching Letter!

Trace and match the Lowercase Letter with its Uppercase Letter in each row.

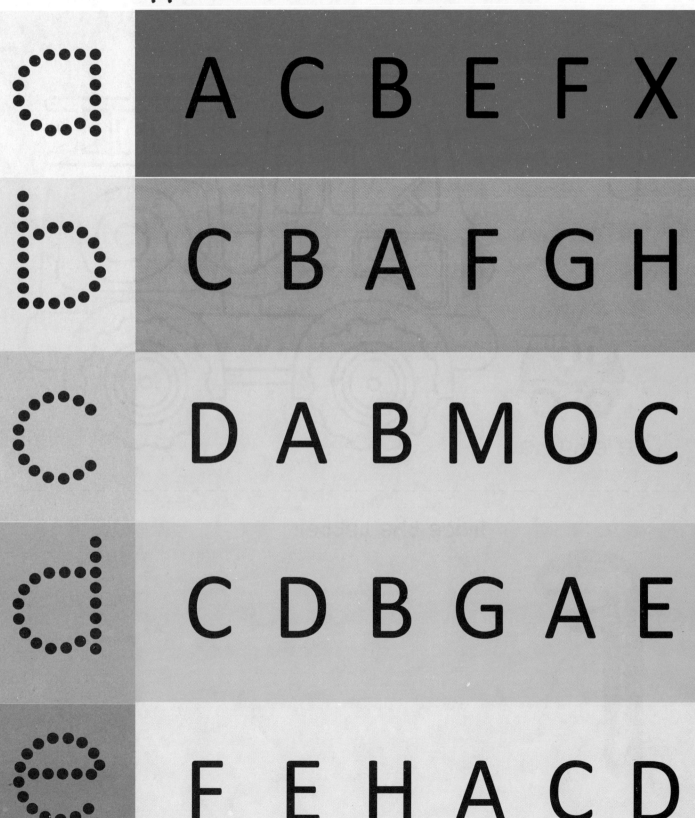

a	A C B E F X
b	C B A F G H
c	D A B M O C
d	C D B G A E
e	F E H A C D

f for fire engine

Color the letter **f** and the **fire engine** brightly.

fire engine

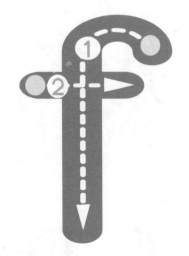

Trace the letter.

f f f f f

f f f f f

g 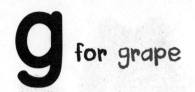 for grape

Color the letter g and the grapes brightly.

g

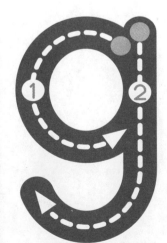

grape

Trace the Letter.

g   g   g   g   g

g   g   g   g   g

 **for hat**

Color the letter h and the hat brightly.

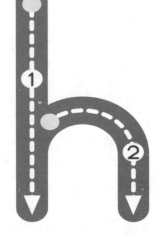

hat

Trace the letter.

h   h   h   h   h

h   h   h   h   h

i for ice cream

Color the letter i and the ice cream brightly.

i

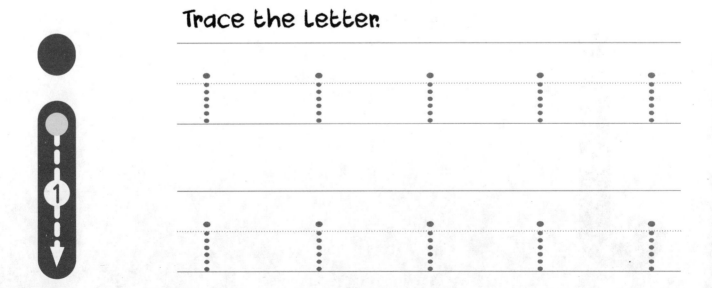

ice cream

Trace the letter.

1

j for jet

Color the letter j and the jet brightly.

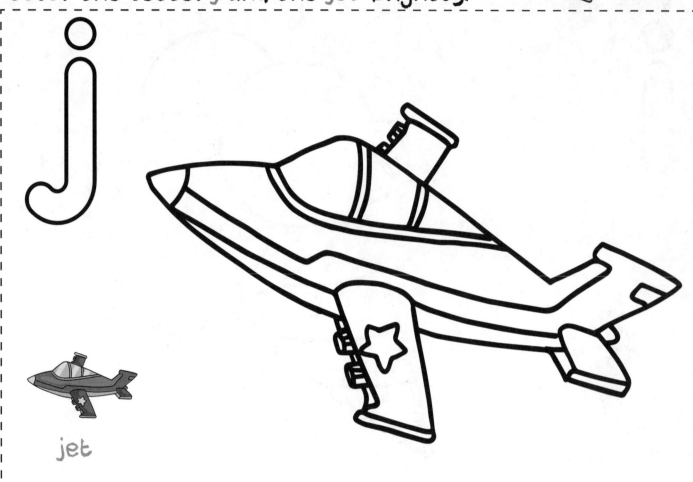

jet

Trace the Letter.

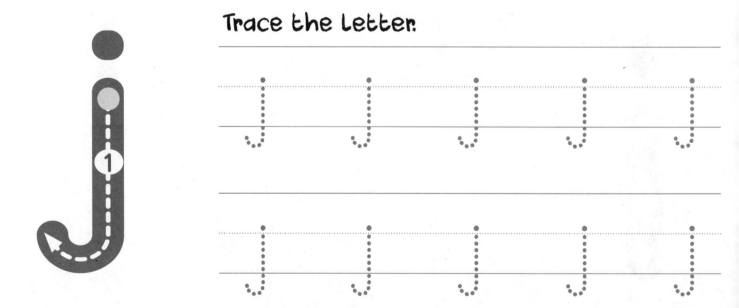

Match Them Up!

Trace the given letters and match with the correct picture.

Find the First Letter!

Circle the beginning letter of each picture.

g h f

i j h

j i g

h j g

Circle the Matching Letter!

Trace and match the Lowercase Letter with its Uppercase Letter in each row.

f	F G H E A J
g	A H G B C D
h	H D O N P X
i	G I D C A S
j	H U T J G F

k for kettle

Color the letter **k** and the **kettle** brightly.

kettle

Trace the letter.

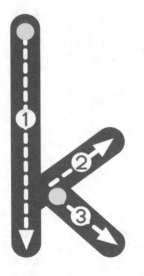

k k k k k

k k k k k

l for Lamp

Color the letter L and the Lamp brightly.

Lamp

Trace the letter.

m for mango

Color the letter m and the mango brightly.

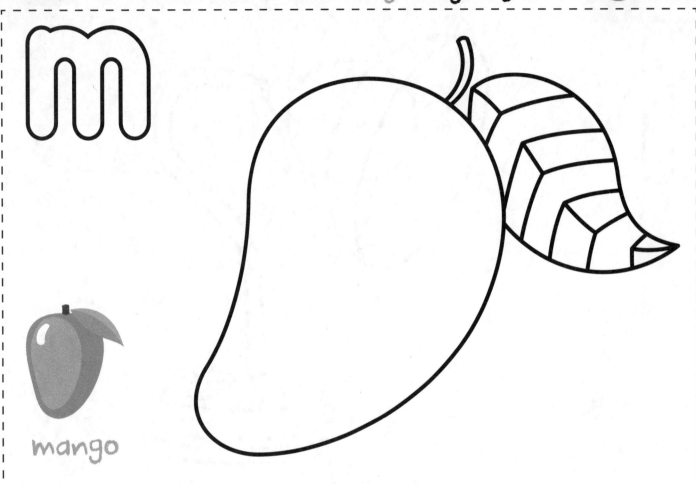

m

mango

Trace the letter.

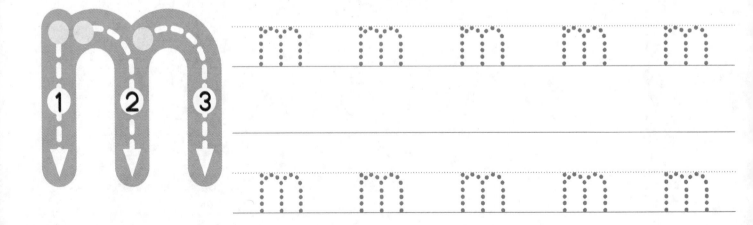

m   m   m   m   m

m   m   m   m   m

n for necklace

Color the letter n and the necklace brightly.

necklace

Trace the letter.

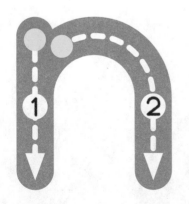

n   n   n   n   n

n   n   n   n   n

O for orange

Color the letter o and the orange brightly.

orange

Trace the letter.

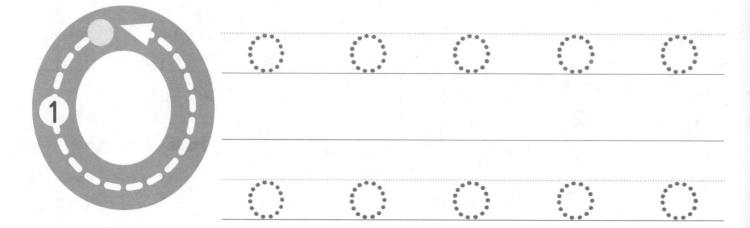

Match Them Up!

Trace the given letters and match with the correct picture.

Find the First Letter!

Circle the beginning letter of each picture.

k m o

n o l

m o k

n m o

Circle the Matching Letter!

Trace and match the Lowercase Letter with its Uppercase Letter in each row.

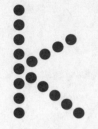 A V K X V G

 L O H J C A

 N M O J W R

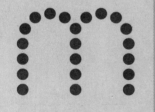 M B N Z A S

 D O P Q G S

 **p** for pizza

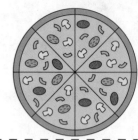

Color the letter p and the pizza brightly.

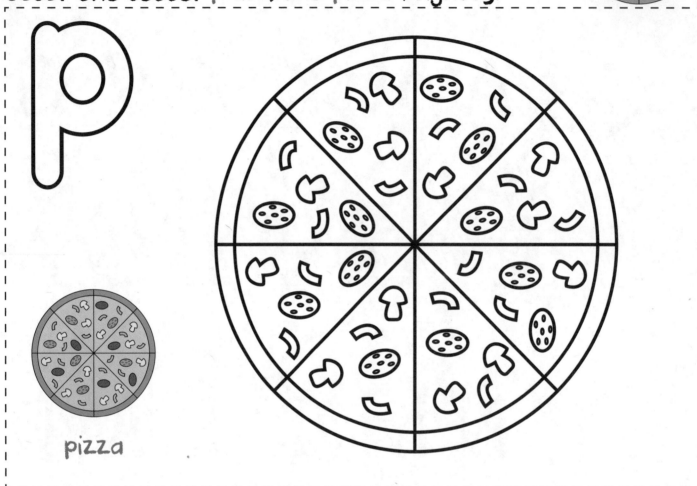

pizza

Trace the Letter.

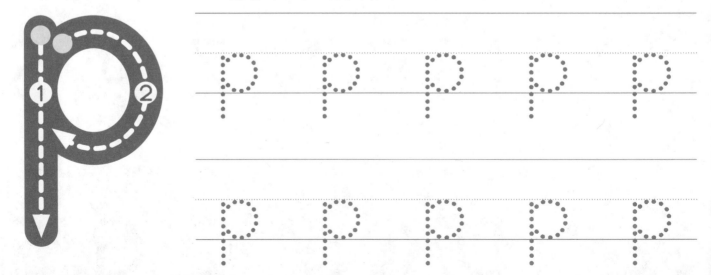

 for queen

Color the letter q and the queen brightly.

queen

Trace the letter.

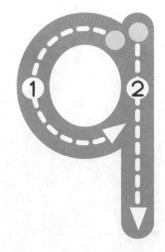

q   q   q   q   q

q   q   q   q   q

r for rose

Color the letter r and the rose brightly.

rose

Trace the letter.

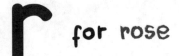

r   r   r   r   r

r   r   r   r   r

S for shoes

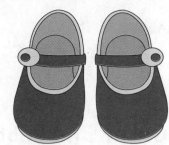

Color the letter s and the shoes brightly.

S

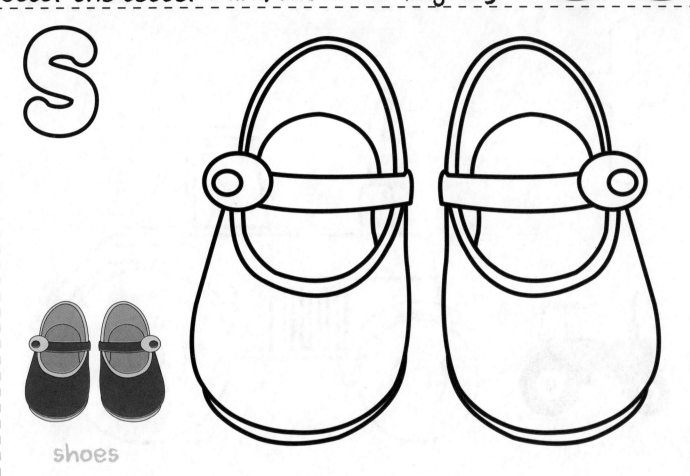

shoes

Trace the letter.

S S S S S

S S S S S

t 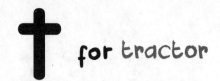 for tractor

Color the letter t and the tractor brightly.

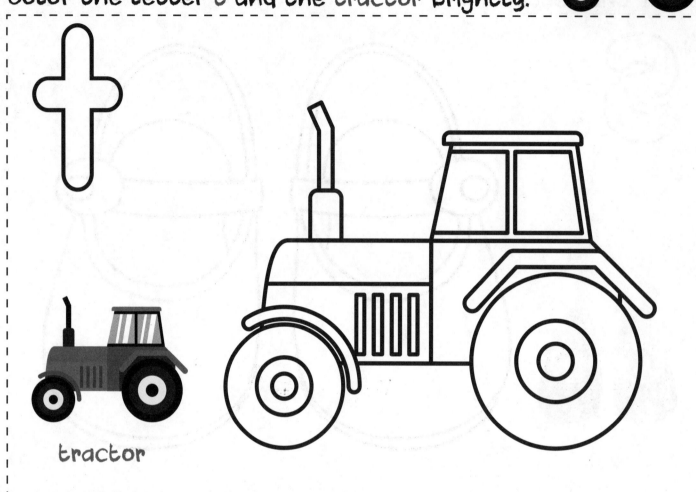

tractor

Trace the letter.

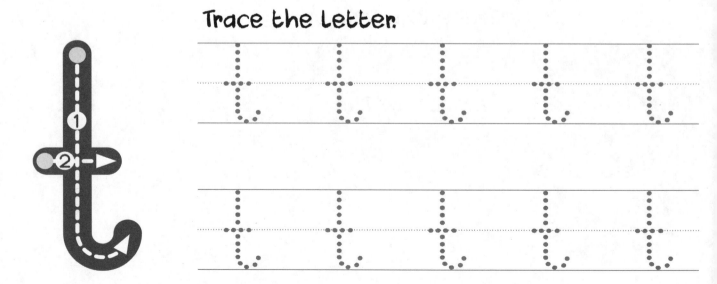

Match Them Up!

Trace the given letters and match with the correct picture.

Find the First Letter!

Circle the beginning letter of each picture.

p r q

q s r

q r s

p t s

Circle the Matching Letter!

Trace and match the Lowercase Letter with its Uppercase Letter in each row.

p	D C P B R G
q	Q O U P D A
r	P Q R B D R
s	S C E Z B U
t	T H F L E B

u for umbrella

Color the letter u and the umbrella brightly.

umbrella

Trace the letter.

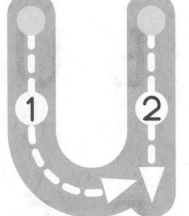

U   U   U   U   U

U   U   U   U   U

V for vase

Color the letter v and the vase brightly.

V

vase

Trace the letter.

V   V   V   V   V

V   V   V   V   V

W  for watermelon

Color the letter **w** and the **watermelon** brightly.

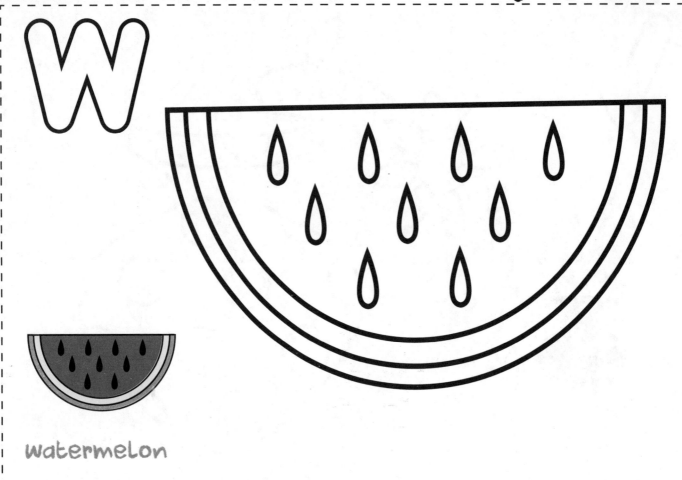

watermelon

Trace the letter.

w   w   w   w   w

w   w   w   w   w

X for xylophone

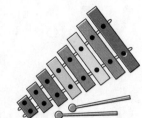

Color the letter x and the xylophone brightly.

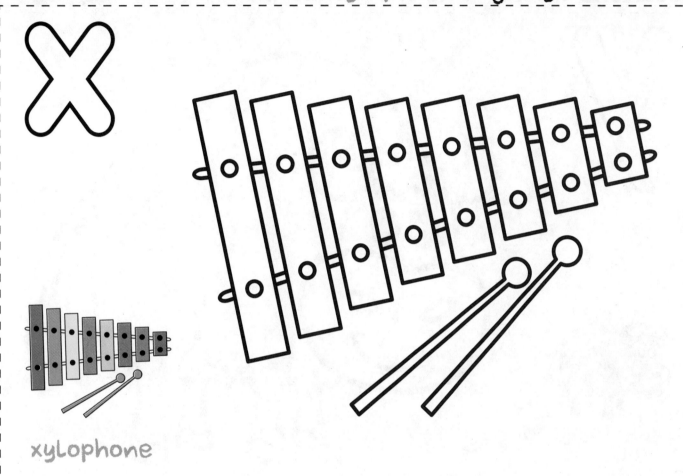

xylophone

Trace the letter.

X X X X X

X X X X X

Y for yak

Color the letter y and the yak brightly.

yak

Trace the letter.

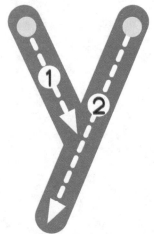

Y Y Y Y Y

Y Y Y Y Y

Z for zebra

Color the letter Z and the zebra brightly.

Z

zebra

Trace the letter.

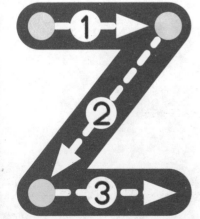

Z Z Z Z Z

Z Z Z Z Z

Match Them Up!

Trace the given letters and match with the correct picture.

Find the First Letter!

Circle the beginning letter of each picture.

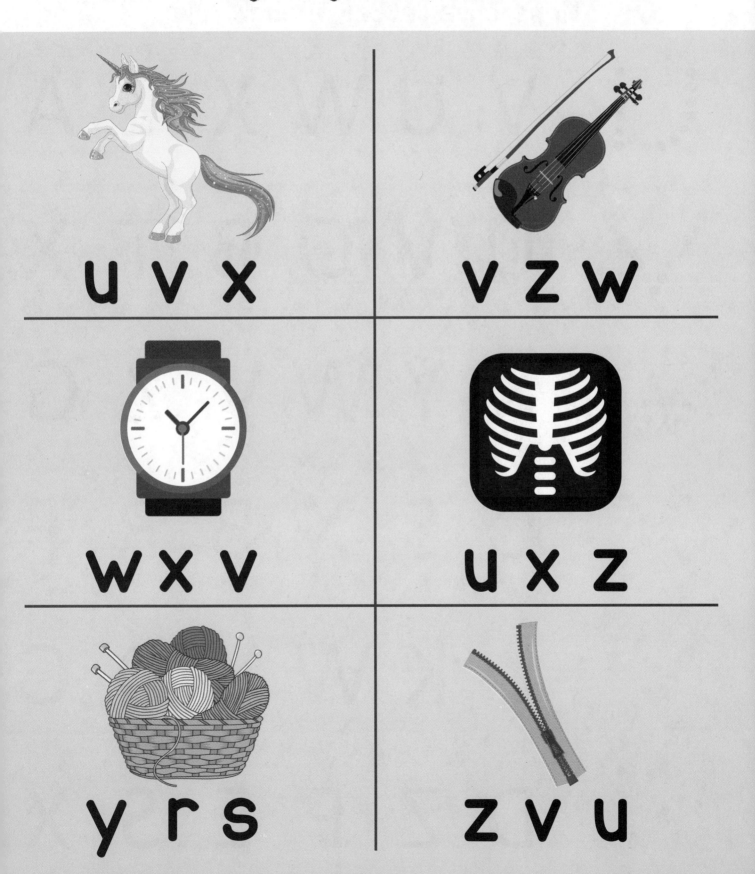

u v x

v z w

w x v

u x z

y r s

z v u

Circle the Matching Letter!

Trace and match the Lowercase Letter with its Uppercase Letter in each row.

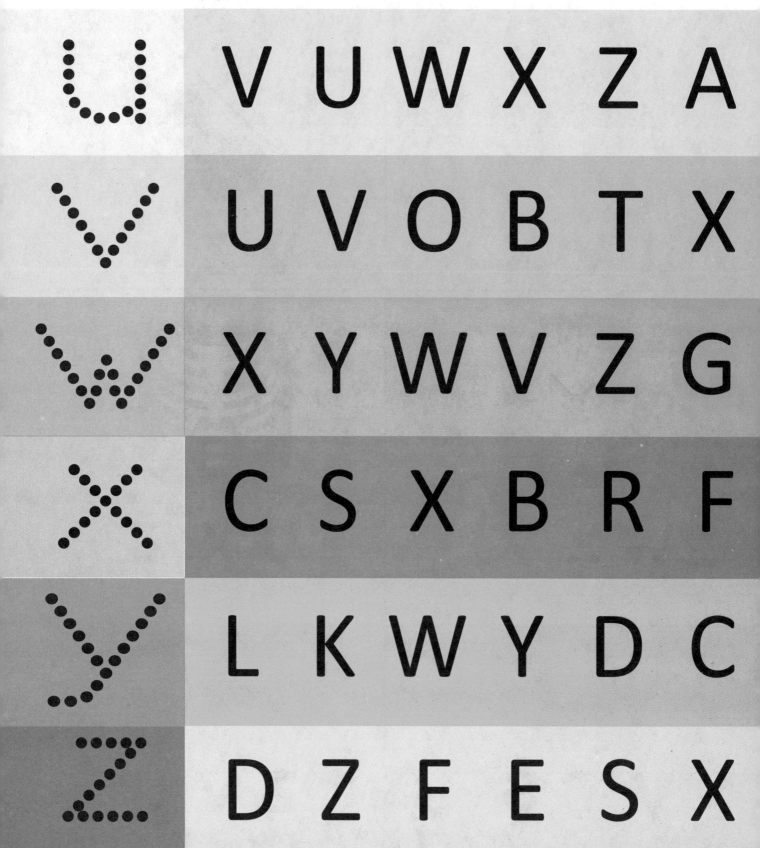

u	V U W X Z A
v	U V O B T X
w	X Y W V Z G
x	C S X B R F
y	L K W Y D C
z	D Z F E S X

abc Maze!

Draw a line along the abc path till z and take the kitten to its favourite food.

Let's See if You Remember!

Trace the lowercase and uppercase letters of the alphabet and say them aloud.

Write the Missing Letters!

Fill the blanks with the missing letters.

ANSWERS

Match Them Up!
Trace the given Letters and match with the correct picture.

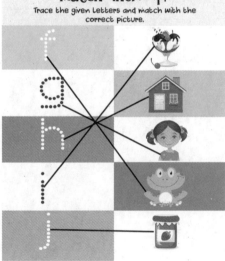

a
b
c
d
e

Find the First Letter!
Circle the beginning Letter for each picture.

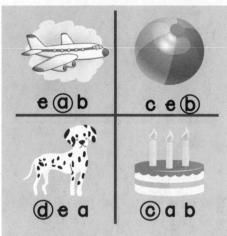

e (a) b   c e (b)

(d) e a   (c) a b

Circle the Matching Letter!
Trace and match the Lowercase Letter with its Uppercase Letter in each row.

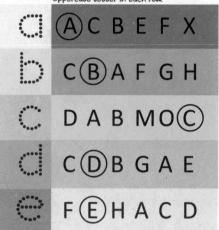

a   (A) C B E F X
b   C (B) A F G H
c   D A B M O (C)
d   C (D) B G A E
e   F (E) H A C D

Match Them Up!
Trace the given Letters and match with the correct picture.

f
g
h
i
j

Find the First Letter!
Circle the beginning Letter for each picture.

(g) h f   i j (h)

j (i) g   h (j) g

Circle the Matching Letter!
Trace and match the Lowercase Letter with its Uppercase Letter in each row.

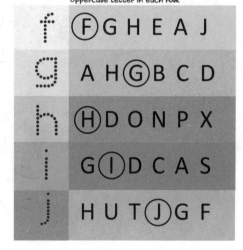

f   (F) G H E A J
g   A H (G) B C D
h   (H) D O N P X
i   G (I) D C A S
j   H U T (J) G F

Match Them Up!
Trace the given Letters and match with the correct picture.

k
l
m
n
o

Find the First Letter!
Circle the beginning Letter for each picture.

(k) m o   n o (l)

(m) o k   (n) m o

Circle the Matching Letter!
Trace and match the Lowercase Letter with its Uppercase Letter in each row.

k   A V (K) X V G
l   (L) O H J C A
m   N (M) O J W R
n   M B (N) Z A S
o   D (O) P Q G S

ANSWERS

Match Them Up!
Trace the given Letters and match with the correct picture.

Find the First Letter!
Circle the begining Letter for each picture.

(p) r q   (q) s r

q (r) s   p t (s)

Circle the Matching Letter!
Trace and match the Lowercase Letter with its Uppercase Letter in each row.

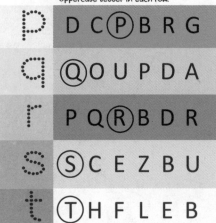

p	D C (P) B R G
q	(Q) O U P D A
r	P Q (R) B D R
s	(S) C E Z B U
t	(T) H F L E B

Match Them Up!
Trace the given Letters and match with the correct picture.

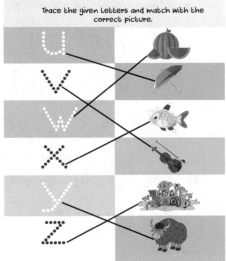

Find the First Letter!
Circle the begining Letter for each picture.

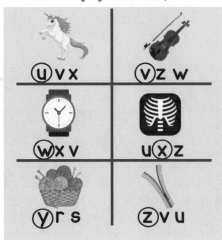

(u) v x   (v) z w

(w) x v   u (x) z

(y) r s   (z) v u

Circle the Matching Letter!
Trace and match the Lowercase Letter with its Uppercase Letter in each row.

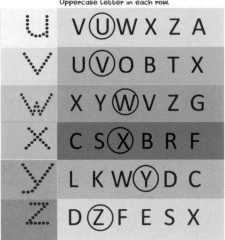

u	V (U) W X Z A
v	U (V) O B T X
w	X Y (W) V Z G
x	C S (X) B R F
y	L K W (Y) D C
z	D (Z) F E S X

abc Maze!
Draw Line along the abc path till z and take the kitten to its favourite food.

Write the Missing Letters!
Fill the blanks with the missing Letters.

a b c d e
f g h i
j k l m n
o p q r
s t u v w
x y z